A Political Fable

★ A ★
POLITICAL
FABLE

Robert Coover

The Viking Press ★ New York

For Diana and Sara:
We read it all by ourselves . . .

First published in 1980 by The Viking Press
625 Madison Avenue, New York, N.Y. 10022
Published simultaneously in Canada by
Penguin Books Canada Limited
"A Political Fable" appeared originally in slightly
different form in *New American Review* under the
title "The Cat in the Hat for President."

LIBRARY OF CONGRESS CATALOGING IN PUBLICATION DATA
Coover, Robert.
A political fable.   I. Title.
PZ4.C78Po   [PS3553.O633]   813.54   80-13623
ISBN 0-670-56309-9

Printed in the United States of America
Set in Bodoni Book

Grateful acknowledgment is made to Random House, Inc.
for permission to reprint a selection from *One Fish, Two
Fish, Red Fish, Blue Fish* by Dr. Seuss. Copyright © 1960
by Dr. Seuss.

Look what we found
in the park
in the dark.
We will take him home.
We will call him Clark.

He will live at our house
He will grow and grow.
Will our mother like this?
We don't know.

—Dr. Seuss,
One Fish, Two Fish,
Red Fish, Blue Fish

A Political Fable

"Why do you sit there like that?" asked the Cat in the Hat.

We stared back at him. The sonuvabitch was unconscious.

> "Lift your chin
> Out of your shoes!
> We will win
> And they will lose!"

Ned held the phone receiver like a club, glared at the Cat, his temples throbbing. What in August and September had looked like the political upset of the century, had by mid-October become a total disaster, not only for our party, but for the nation as well.

"Some news is glad,
Some news is sad,
I do not think—"

"Shove it," snapped Joe. Ned dropped the phone receiver to its cradle with a bang. Our party's moderates and liberals, so-called, my men Riley and Boone among them, had just pulled out, leaving us stranded, to form a rump group in support of the Opponent. It was a move almost unprecedented in the history of American politics. So was the more serious threat that lay behind it.

Sam, pacing, paused to clap one hand to the Cat's shoulder and suggest quietly that he go for a walk or take a nap or something. But the Cat remained, grinning foolishly. Sam shrugged, resumed his pacing.

I watched Clark. Clark watched us. Benignly, hugely, over thin hands folded just under his eyes. He more than anyone had brought us to this strange crisis. Yet he betrayed no surprise, no solutions, no remorse.

Joe took a hard drag on his cigarette, ground it out savagely in an ashtray. "Well, we've gotta think of something and damn quick," he snapped.

The Cat doffed his Hat and out popped a Something that commenced to dash preposterously around the room. Infuriated, Ned leaped up and stomped on it. *"Get your silly ass outa here!"* he screamed at the Cat, and kicked him out the door. Ned was an affable guy, circumspect and deferential. His reckless boot in the butt of our party's nominee for the next President of the United States of America only showed how bad things really were.

I could have said, I told you so, but it was no time for that either. Nor for that matter was it necessary. It was clear they all remembered my early opposition—an opposition that had nearly cost me my job—remembered it and now counted it wisdom, for much of the decision-making was falling on my shoulders again. "Your ball, Sooth," Joe said. Given the nature of the decisions that lay ahead, I can't say I was all that happy about it.

In truth, my original objections to the Cat in the Hat had been of a merely practical sort. I'd been convinced from the outset of the impossibility of unseating the incumbent party this year: a war was on and the nation was prosperous. As I saw it, our job was to build for the elections four years hence, and I accepted the National Chairmanship of the party in that spirit. I was convinced we had to strengthen and enlarge the center to win, and therefore sought the nomination of a solid middle-of-the-roader with an uncontroversial record, a man whose carefully controlled candidacy this year would lay the groundwork for his election four years later.

Moreover, even had we, not they, been the party in power, the Opponent would have been a tough man to beat. Born in a small Midwestern town of middle-class parents, reared and educated in the Southwest, known to have considerable holdings and influence in the Eastern Establishment, a poker buddy of several Southern Senators, progressive and city-oriented yet bluntly individualistic and rural in manner, rugged, shrewd, folksy, taciturn yet gregarious, a member of everything from SANE and the NAACP to the American Legion, Southern Baptists, and the National Association of Manufacturers, a chameleon personality who could project the faces of Chairman of the Board, Sheriff, Sunday Duffer, Private Eye, Young Man on the Go, Cracker-barrel Philosopher, Lion-tamer, Dad, Quarterback, Country Gentleman, City Lawyer, Good Sport, Field General, Swinger, and the Guy Next Door, all in one three-minute TV sequence, the Opponent was, in short, a natural. Of course, as Clark was to point out and the Cat to demonstrate, he was not without serious failings, what man is? But when I took over in early spring as the minority party's National Chairman, it was generally conceded he was a shoo-in. Later, at their Convention, a young, soft-spoken, Harvard-educated New York Congressman was chosen as his running mate. Beautiful. Christ, how I envied them!

There are risk-takers in politics, bold men who wait their chance then go for broke, latent Hotspurs suddenly gunning for immortality with the intensity and single-mindedness of an assassin or a saint. I'm proud to say I'm not one of them. My life in business and politics has been long, successful, and colorless. I have been, among other things, a state senator and treasurer, a U.S. Congressman, an undersecretary in the Department of Commerce, and Ambassador to Costa Rica, but most of my political life has been spent—in and around business—working quietly for the party. I could no longer count the number of ad hoc committees I've chaired, closed sessions swayed, anonymous tasks performed. Without headlines, without glory —though not without honor. It was a tribute to my effectiveness that the press, upon receiving news of my appointment, merely

took it for granted. MR. BROWN NAMED
PARTY HEAD.

Theoretically, politics is all issues: the
word used to describe the conflicts arising
in men's efforts to suffer one another. But
practically, of course, there are no issues in
politics at all. Not even ideological species.
"Liberal," "conservative," "left," "right,"
these are mere fictions of the press, meta-
phoric conventions to which politicians
sooner or later and in varying ways adapt.
Politics in a republic is a complex pattern
of vectors, some fixed and explicable, some
random, some bullish, some inchoate and
permutable, some hidden and dynamic,
others celebrated though flagging, usually
collective, sometimes even cosmic—and a
politician's job is to know them and ride
them. So instinctive has my perception of
the kinetics of politics been, so accurate my
forecasts of election outcomes, I have come
to be known jocularly as Soothsayer Brown
among my colleagues, or, more spitefully,
Gypsy.

I even foresaw, many campaigns ago, what most men cannot: my own electoral defeat—foresaw it, accepted it, and then willingly took on the scapegoat's role by espousing a number of unpopular minority views to help broaden the party's base. I've been called a "liberal" in the media ever since: I! who own twenty suits, all in obscure shades of brown, and who in over forty years of eating in restaurants of every category and cuisine have yet to order anything except hamburger steak, charred to a crisp. You see, I am blessed—or damned, as you will—with puffy pink lips. They helped me to win my seat in the House of Representatives, just as later they helped me to lose it. My short stature, round belly, smooth pink scalp, anonymous name, and occasionally irascible temper no doubt contributed, but mainly it was the fat lips. By thrusting the lower one forward, I was able to project a marvelous complexion of self-righteous anger, a kind of holy Bible-belting zeal for judgment, which complemented nicely the central issue, so-called, of my winning campaign: an attack on my incumbent opponent's corruption. That wonderful pout did me little service, however, in defending myself against the same attacks two years later. Anybody with lips like that, you knew, just had to blow it. Of course, there were many factors, many vectors, but the fat lips were decisive. "Greatness" in American politics has always been associated with thin lips—some obscure racial or iconic bias, no doubt—and there was nothing I could do about it. I predicted my young tight-lipped challenger would take 56 percent of the vote; he won 56.4 percent.

And so, many years, many engagements, many auguries later, now chairmaning my party and confronting an apparently invincible Opponent, publicly proclaiming an upset victory in November, whoever our candidate might be, but privately seeking a candidate to fit the probable vectors of the campaign four years hence, I could only react with bitterness and frustration to the Convention-floor move by a clutch of zany young turks to nominate the Cat in the Hat. Every man has his weakness and I have mine: my own failing, as perhaps you've already noticed, is a limited sense of humor. It has flawed my campaigns, curtailed my diplomatic career, been the blind spot in my perception of political dynamics. Rationally, I accept the idea that life is at best a game, yet my nature is serious and fiercely competitive: I fight to win and couldn't help it if I would. The Cat in the Hat campaign buttons appeared the second day of the National Convention, provoking a general merriment. As the laughter mounted, I grew uneasy, then irritable, finally incensed. Not until the Convention was nearly over—and then only thanks to Clark—did I discover the significance of that laughter. Soothsayer or no, I was the last to embrace the Cat and wear the badge.

Not only, you see, had I succeeded in finding the ideal candidate for my long-range, plans, I had found two: a spirited Irish Protestant from Boston named Riley, and a tall lantern-jawed Westerner named

Boone, direct descendant of the romantic frontiersman. I delight in the illusion of democracy in action, not only because it wins votes but also for its own sake. An open contest between two well-chosen candidates is a great entertainment, an exciting relaxation from the real work of politics. There are risks, of course, especially in intraparty matches such as the one I was arranging. A deadlock could occur, for example, bringing about the nomination of a dark horse—or a dark cat, to speak to our case. But, given the virtual inevitability of losing the elections this year, even that possibility did not seem entirely undesirable: Riley and Boone would get all the pre-Convention publicity, one of them would probably be the Vice-Presidential candidate, the dark-horse Presidential contestant would bear the onus of defeat, and my two men would again be going for the top spot four years later, then as seasoned and respected veterans. So I organized support teams for them in all fifty states, secured sizable campaign funds for each, through friendly media outlets elevated them from anonymity to world fame almost overnight, encouraged and directed their participation in selected state primaries, brought them onto the Convention floor in a final rush of electoral fever, drama, and glory—and all for nothing. Once the Cat took over, they somehow looked like fools.

"I CAN LEAD IT ALL BY MYSELF" was the legend on the Cat's campaign buttons. His button portrait was the familiar one: tall floppy red-and-white striped hat, red bow tie, white-gloved hands clasped decorously over his chest, thumbs pressed together, grinning that idiot grin (though thin-lipped, I had to admit). The Cat in the Hat himself did not at first appear. His madcap explosion on the scene was engineered—apparently, at least—by Joe and Ned, a couple of maverick Midwesterners whose techniques were as fresh as they were amateurish. Only several hysterical hours later was I to meet the real spirit behind the coup:

a luminous, ingenious, pear-shaped mass named Clark.

The first day went as I'd planned, with plenty of fanfare, good food and drink, back-slapping and vote-trading, stirring speeches, the usual Convention hoopla—though admittedly it was all a little hollow, beclouded with the factuality of being the party out of power and little or no hope of getting in. The only hint of something out of order was the slogan that appeared on toilet walls and crept oddly into conversations: "Let's make the White House a Cat House." But the next morning, into the hotel breakfast rooms throughout the city, Joe and Ned, dressed like the Cat in striped hat, bow tie, and gloves, came shuffling, doing a soft-shoe to their "Cat in the Hat Campaign Song":

It is no time for no, it is time for yes!
It is time to elect our candidate!
Here is the Cat who will clean up the mess:
The Cat in the Hat for the Head of State!

So go to bat for the Cat in the Hat!
He's the Cat who knows where it's at!
With Tricks and Voom and Things
    like that!
Go! Go! The Cat in the Hat!

They passed out buttons, introduced the
Cat-Call (*Me-You!*), and yak-yakked their
way through a cornball vaudeville routine
with such awful gags as:

JOE: Hello! Hello!
NED: I said hello! Can you hear me,
Joe?
JOE: What is this, a party line?
NED: Well, that's what I'm calling
about, Mr. Joe!—to tell you about our
new party line!
JOE: What line is that, Mr. Ned?
NED: Why, a *Fe*-line, Mr. Joe! I'm
talking about the next President of the
United States!
JOE: The next President! Who's that,
Mr. Ned?
NED: Why, it's the Cat in the Hat!

JOE: I'm sorry, Mr. Ned, I didn't get your predicate . . . ?

NED: A pretty cat? Well, no, he ain't so pretty, Mr. Joe, but he's got a lotta *pussy-nality!*

JOE *and* NED *sing the "Cat in the Hat Campaign Song" while passing out buttons, then soft-shoe out.*

It is no time to fear, it is time to cheer!
It is time to play on your instrument!
The New Day is near, the New Way
   is here!
The Cat in the Hat for President!

   So go to bat for the Cat in the Hat!
   He's the Cat who knows where it's at!
   With Tricks and Voom and Things
      like that!
   Go! Go! The Cat in the Hat!

By evening my beautifully planned Convention had turned into something of a circus. Regardless of political commitments, nearly everyone had taken to singing the Cat in the Hat song, and, even alongside their other pins, to wearing the Cat

button—I even caught my man Riley with
one of the damned things on. On the toilet
walls: "What This Nation Needs Is More
Pussy!" And sure enough, at the banquet
that night, in pranced a hundred gorgeous
milk-fed Midwestern co-eds, dressed in tight
elastic catskins, wearing the goofy hat, bow
tie, and gloves, leaping in and out of laps
and licking faces, sending up a delicious
caterwaul of *Me-You's*. The new gimmick
of the night was a miniature replica of the
Cat's Hat with an elastic band for fastening
under the chin—when you squeezed the
Hat, it emitted the Cat-Call. "Keep it under
your hat!" the girls purred as they passed
them out, then whisked away, twirling their
tails. For some reason, everyone kept grinning at me, apparently conjecturing that
I'd arranged the whole gag, and since I still
wasn't sure just what was up, I grinned
along with them, returned their winks, even
—though only one time—squeezed the silly
Hat.

The Cat in the Hat himself appeared a
day later right in the middle of my man

Boone's big parade and rally, breaking it
up. It's against tradition for a candidate to
appear on the Convention floor before his
final nomination. It's against all propriety
to intrude on another candidate's rally. And
the Cat's performance itself was against
every standard of Convention-floor behav-
ior, not to say all probability. But that
damned Cat couldn't care less—in fact, this
balmy flaunting of the rules of the game was
to become the pattern, if not in fact the
message, of his whole Presidential campaign.

Boone, a Californian, had been nominated by the Governor of Kentucky, with
handsome seconds from Alaska, Virginia,
California, and Idaho. I was delighted. His
symbols were coonskin caps (Boone-skins,
his supporters were calling them) and b'ar
guns (in fact, before politics, he'd been a
chemist and later vice-president of one of
the nation's largest pharmaceutical com-
panies, had never had any kind of gun in
his hands before in his life); his slogans:
"Explore the moon with Boone!" and "We

want Boone *soon!*" A thousand frenetic, hollering, coonskin-capped, placard- and flag-waggling, bull-roaring, Madison-Avenue-b'ar-gun-toting demonstrators had piled in, pushed wildly to the front, seized the microphones to broadcast their chants, looking like they might decide to take the Convention by force, when the Cat in the Hat turned up. Clinking and clanking in on that goofy clean-up machine of his, the machine now bearing in red-white-and-blue letters his famous line: "HAVE NO FEAR OF THIS MESS!"

Maybe the Boone people thought the Cat was one of their own—certainly he was lugging a rusty old b'ar gun over what he had of a shoulder. At any rate, they went suddenly silent, quick as it takes to snap off the TV, and turned expectantly to the Cat, who said:

> "Hello! hello!
> How are you?
> Can you do
> What I can do?"

Arms reached out from the clean-up machine, snatching Boone posters. The Cat shuffled them, passed them out again. Now they read: "Eat a prune at noon with Boone!"

Another mechanical arm stretched forth and from the crowd plucked, by the seat of his honorable pants, Boone's nominator, the Governor of the State of Kentucky, by image a rotund dignified Southern gentleman, already looking a little out of character in his Boone-skin cap, much more so now dangling, rump-high, over the Convention floor, the tail of his cap down between his eyes. The Cat in the Hat lowered him to the platform, whisked off his coonskin cap. Under it was another, oddly a bit larger than the first. The Cat pulled this one off, revealing yet another, larger still. The next coonskin lay on the Governor's ears, the next flopped down over his eyes. As the Cat whisked off caps, the Governor gradually disappeared beneath them. Soon he was wearing a cap that covered his head and rested on his shoulders, then one that flopped down his shirt front, others that lay on his plump belly, reached to his knees, his shoes, until finally there was only one huge coonskin cap on the platform. The Cat lifted the cap: no Governor! Shouts of amazement, even fright, from the Convention floor. The Cat, though smiling still, looked perplexed. Silence fell. The Cat doffed his own Hat, and there, on his head, in the lotus position, sat the Governor of Kentucky. *"Me-You!"* the Governor said, then clapped a pudgy hand over his mouth, gazed sheepishly at the now wildly cheering, wildly hooting crowd.

The Cat fired his b'ar gun suddenly, a tremendous explosion and cloud of smoke: when it cleared, all the Boone-skins had turned into live raccoons which were scampering madly about, sending the girls shrieking up onto chairs with lifted skirts. Sure enough, under most of the Boone-skins, the delegates had been wearing the miniature Cat Hats, which they now merrily squeezed, raising a din of happy Cat-Calls.

Some of the coons balanced balls on their noses, some rolled and tumbled, but most of them started humping each other. The whole nationally televised Convention floor was a mad melee of shrieking laughing girls, Cat-Hat-squeezing delegates, and copulating coons. I fainted dead away. Later, they told me that the Cat fired one final salvo on his b'ar gun, and a little flag popped out that said:

> "Come along!
> Follow me!
> Don't be afraid!
> There are many more games
> That we haven't yet played!"

And then he'd clinkclanked out of the hall in his clean-up machine, the Governor of Kentucky squeezed, wide-eyed and jolly, in beside him, most of the delegates deliriously *Me-Youing* along in his wake.

Riley never even got nominated. It took hours to clear the hall of coons—in fact, as far as I know, they've got the run of the place yet—and anyway the delegates never came back. In the media nothing but the Cat in the Hat: he was a national sensation, though the media people themselves, infected by it all, were filing haphazard and even outrageous stories. The Cat, though in great demand, slipped out of sight, but his disruptive spirit lingered on. The delegates were completely out of hand, and the banquets that night were slapstick, table-dumping, pie-throwing affairs. Only one of my scheduled speakers had the nerve to carry on—someone rigged his mike through a tape recorder so that everything came out backwards; when he paused, his scrambled voice carried on, and when he spoke the speakers went silent. "What's happening?" he cried and sat down abruptly on a miniature Cat Hat someone had planted in his chair, issuing a lusty *ME-YOU!*—had a heart attack, and nearly died. Things were that serious. And through it all shuffled Ned and Joe with their lame-brain hayseed routines:

NED: Say, Mr. Joe, our nation has got *cat* problems!

JOE: How do you mean, *cat* problems, Mr. Ned? Can you make me a list?

NED: Make you a *list?* Why, Mr. Joe, I'll make you a *catty*-log!

JOE *smiles as the audience guffaws and issues the Cat-Call.*

NED: I mean, things is catty-clysmic, Mr. Joe. They are catty-plectic, catty-strophic, and all cattywamptious!

JOE: That bad, hunh? Well, what're we gonna do about it, Mr. Ned?

NED: Well, Mr. Joe, I say you gotta send a cat in to do a cat's job.

JOE: Send a cat in to do a cat's job? How do you mean, Mr. Ned?

NED: Well, Mr. Joe, supposing *your* house was full of rats, what would *you* do?

JOE: Unh-hunh, I think I see what you mean, Mr. Ned! The Cat in the Hat for President sounds like a good idea . . .

NED: It's not just a good idea, Mr. Joe —it's a *catty-gorical im-purr-ative!*

As I knew sooner or later they would, they cornered me. Intermediaries arranged it. In a locked hotel room. Darkened, shades pulled. Forty-buck fifth of whiskey between us. With them, to my astonishment, was my old friend Sam, popular Governor of a Northwestern state and a Favorite Son candidate for the Presidential nomination, one of the men I'd counted on to break any possible deadlock between Riley and Boone. All three tense and serious, no comedy now.

At a late-afternoon press conference, I'd issued some pretty harsh statements about the Cat. His forces, most vocally Ned and Joe, had countered with accusations of king-making and obstructionism and even senility. Attempting that evening to put my Convention back together again, I'd discovered a terrible foolishness, a vast derision, a widespread breakdown of all I'd considered solid and meaningful in American politics. As far as I could tell, Riley and Boone were not so much running neck and neck as skidding rump and rump. In a desperate gesture, I'd pressured Boone into agreeing to throw his support to Riley upon the latter's expected nomination the next day, but it was no longer certain Boone *had* any support. I'd sought out the Favorite Sons, but most of them were wearing those silly little Cat Hats and chasing drunkenly after the catskinned co-eds. The sane ones left had seemed to be clustering around my friend Sam, as I'd hoped, but Sam was nowhere to be found. When I encountered him at last, in the locked hotel room, cheek by jowl with Joe and Ned, I knew that all was lost. The laws in Sam's state forbade his running for reelection and he had no chance for the Senate. I knew that, more than anything else, he wanted to be Secretary of State, and I figured he'd made his deal. But I hadn't made mine, and I wasn't about to.

In spite of their attacks and the reported rumors I was soon to be dumped, I knew they needed me—needed my long experience, my innumerable contacts, the accumulation of favors owed me, my weight with party regulars, my notorious capacity for political prophecy. As for my part, I didn't need them so much as I needed their absence. But I respected their sudden power and knew I'd have to negotiate. I was trying my damnedest to see Joe as a Vice-President, Ned as Secretary of Agriculture or something. As a result, we never really got on the same circuit. As we drank, Joe was talking about air power and the Red menace, Ned about technology and history, and I was trying to pry out of them what they wanted for themselves. Finally, I turned to Sam. "What are you doing here?" I asked him.

"Well, as you know, Sooth," said Sam, who was, almost ineluctably, to get tagged Sam-I-Am by the media in the campaign to come, "I live existentially. I'm not as confident as these fellows are that the Cat is going to be our next President, but I do believe nobody else is going to get nominated by our party. For good or bad, Sooth, we've got to accept the Cat's success and timing."

I grunted depreciatively. I knew he was right. But I was too disgusted to admit it.

"Besides, as I've learned, the Cat has many virtues. He's fresh and original, and famous, too. A whole new generation of voters, Sooth, has grown up on his tales. He's a living legend."

"So is Woody Woodpecker," I said grumpily.

Sam smiled. "Well, okay, he's something of a nut, it's true, or at least that's the way he chooses to come on. Yet it's a charismatic kind of zaniness, Sooth. He's funny. He's captivating. And ultimately I think he's sane. Did you see what he did to that Convention today?"

"Are you kidding?" I'd seen the replay of my swoon on the six o'clock newscast, and I supposed that Sam had, too. Stuffy, they called me. CAT SHATTERS BROWN'S BORE, said the press. "But, damn it, Sam, what are we running here, a political party or a carnival freak show? You want a deal, I'll make you one. But I won't see my party given over to a bunch of short-sighted crackpots without a fight!"

Sam winced; the others seemed offended. They leaned back. "Let's let him talk to Clark," Joe said.

And so that was how and when I met Clark. Large. Pale. Soft. He emerged from the obscurity of the room like an apparition. He was ugly, stark, nearly expressionless, spoke in a monotone—yet so charged the space around him as to seemingly snuff out the rest of the world. Joe, Sam, and Ned were surely there all the while, but I didn't see them. I recognized my new antagonist intuitively: the political visionary. Suddenly, though still indistinctly, the Cat in the Hat movement took on a new dimension. For one blinding instant, I glimpsed beyond the Cat's antics toward something new and extraordinary, beyond the disruption of National Conventions toward a vast reconstruction of human life. And then, as instantly, it faded. I resent, instinctively, such illusions. "Mr. Brown," he said with a slight nod of his head, but without extending his hand, "they call me Clark."

He sat, or perhaps he was sitting all the

time. There was nothing, directly, to fear from him. Yet I was afraid. My own lucid perception of the vectors of politics was fast dissolving. In self-defense, I got right to the point: "What do you want?"

"A new world, Mr. Brown."

"Full of rutting raccoons," I said derisively.

"We had to work with what you gave us."

"What does a hall full of fucking coons got to do with government?" I asked angrily.

"What does grown twentieth-century men wearing their skins on their heads have to do with government?" he countered.

"It's a metaphor, Clark. That's politics."

"Exactly." A brief smile seemed to flick over his face. "You have a reputation, Mr. Brown, for phenomenally accurate political analysis. Yet not only do you seem unable to understand *why* your metaphor failed and ours worked, you seem unable to accept the simple *fact* that this is what has happened."

"All right," I admitted, "it worked today. Maybe. But tomorrow the building employees will probably be out on strike, refusing to clean up all the coon shit. Then what?"

"If it were necessary, the Cat would have them wallowing in it up to their ears and loving it," said Clark calmly. "Though of course it won't be necessary."

"Okay, okay, I accept the fact. Now what?"

"No, Mr. Brown, I'm afraid you don't. You came here hoping to make a deal. You still hope to make a deal. But the revolution has begun, Mr. Brown. There are no deals to be made."

Something whistled through me like a cold damp wind: illusions, I knew, could blow holes in you. "But what's the Cat in the Hat got to do with your so-called revolution?" I asked with what little sarcasm I could still muster.

"Most immediately, Mr. Brown, the Cat is funny. And dramatic. We have a terrible need for the extraordinary. We are weary of war, weary of the misery under our supposed prosperity, weary of dullness and routine, weary of all the old ideas, weary of all the masks we wear, the roles we play, the foolish games we sustain. The Cat cuts through all this. We laugh. For a moment, we are free."

"Maybe," I said, "but clowns never win elections."

"I see you are still resisting," said Clark. "In your adoration of the past, Mr. Brown, you have isolated yourself from the actual and the possible. It is the great Western disease."

"What? Freedom from illusions?" I asked drily.

"No, history." Clark was utterly imperturbable. Or else he had a worse sense of humor even than I did. "The mystification of history produced by our irrational terror of reality. If you'll pardon the pun, Mr. Brown, we need to perform a kind of racial historectomy on all humankind."

I smiled politely, though Clark did not return it. "So your Cat is going to wield the surgical blade," I said, the smile having soured. "With Tricks and Voom and Things like that." Still, I knew what a random business being was, what a hoax, what a hobble history could be. Hadn't I been thumbing my nose at it all my life with my practiced anonymity? Clark had got to me there.

"He's the first step, Mr. Brown, that's all. Remember, I speak of a total revolution, not merely this election."

"Now you're resisting, Clark. There's still the election to be won. Otherwise, your would-be revolution doesn't get off the ground."

"Perhaps." Clark paused, almost as though he hadn't considered my objection before. "As a famous political analyst, Mr. Brown, what would you say was a politician's greatest asset?"

I paused. In my perception of a field of charged vectors, I tend to deny hierarchies of power. "I don't know," I said finally. "Ambiguity, I guess. Meaningful or potent ambiguity."

"Wonderful!" said Clark, and again that glimmer of a smile flickered for an instant on his pale face. "And what do we know about the Cat in the Hat?"

It had been some time since I'd read the stories to my grandkids. "Two hundred twenty-three different words," I said. It was the kind of thing I'd be apt to remember. Clark said nothing and I didn't like the silence, so I added: "There were these two kids by the window. And the Cat let these two Things out of a box and they flew some kites around in the house making one helluva mess." My grandkids had got a big charge out of that. "The Cat cleaned it up with that machine he used today." When my grandkids tried the kite act, we didn't have a machine. If they'd been my kids, I would've tanned their fannies, but what can a grandfather do? "Then, in the second one, he eats a cake in the bathtub and leaves a pink ring." My grandkids wanted to know why you couldn't see the Cat's peenie while he was standing in the tub. They didn't ask that about any of the other pictures. "Before he's done, everything in sight is pink."

"That's very good, Mr. Brown," said

Clark. A pun on catechism occurred to me, but I swallowed it down. "And this time his solution, after running through an alphabet of cats all residing in his own hat, is—"

"Voom."

"Voom indeed!"

"The Bomb, as Joe has it."

"Yes, it's true," said Clark. "For Joe, the two stories are parables of the foibles of diplomacy, the first being about the effectiveness of air power, followed by technological recovery, the second about the eradication of the, uh, Red menace by atomic power."

"This is what you call freeing the mind."

Again that flicker. Clark's moods were subtle, but I was beginning to appreciate them. "Any dramatic change of the rules of the game, Mr. Brown, is by definition a radical action, and so attracts radicals of all stripes. At any rate, we are speaking as practical politicians now, Mr. Brown, and my purpose is merely to demonstrate the Cat's essential ambiguity, and thus his electoral power."

Mr. Brown, a return to racial sanity. Voom may simply be the reality principle!"

"Well, all that's very cute, Clark," I said, "but there's a lot of destructiveness in those Cat stories. Think of those—"

"But what does it *matter* that there's destructiveness, Mr. Brown? The question is rather: *what* is being destroyed? The Cat breaks the rules of the house, even the laws of probability, but what is destroyed except nay-saying itself, authority, social habit, the law of the mother, who, through violence in the name of love, keeps order in this world, this household? Ah no, mess-making is a prerequisite to creation, Mr. Brown. All new worlds are built upon the ruins of the old."

"Bump, thump," I said, recalling some of the lines. My opposition, nevertheless, was waning.

"And *jump*, Mr. Brown! The leap into the future! *Jump!*"

I sighed. "I'm too old to jump, Clark. Or should I say, too plump in the rump? But

I'm not young enough to stop you all by myself either. What are your terms?"

"You're not listening, Mr. Brown. *There are no terms.* Take, if you like, the existential perspective of your friend Governor Sam. It is *happening,* Mr. Brown. Are you with us or not?"

Revolt, derring-do, mess-making are not my way. I liked my mother. But Clark was right; I saw all the vectors again: it was indeed happening. And anyway, the Cat, I recalled, always cleaned up his own messes. After the liberating infractions, the old rules were restored—reinforced, in fact. Appreciated. "Okay," I said, and poured a long one. I needed it badly. "Here's to the Cat who knows where it's at," I proposed, meaning whomever you please.

The Cat in the Hat was nominated by acclamation before the completion of the first ballot the next day as our party's candidate for the next President of the United States of America. There was some prior debate about the Vice-Presidency. It seemed that the Cat's supporters were prepared to let me have my way in the matter. But I discouraged Riley and Boone from getting mixed up in it—to tell the truth, they'd both started to get a little wacky themselves and broke into wild laughter every time I mentioned the Presidency, but they willingly went along with me, backed the Cat, and withdrew from the game. Finally, we settled on Sam. The way things turned out, I wish I'd talked him out of it, too, but at the time he was too obviously the right choice.

Actually, the nomination and balloting procedures that final day were orderly, just about like any other National Convention, and in spite of the coon odor, I was even beginning to feel at home in the hall again, but then the Cat came on to accept the nomination. He arrived on roller skates, holding up a cake on a rake. On, or in, the cake sat a goat wearing a coat, an umbrella balanced on its nose. On the tip of the umbrella wobbled a fishbowl, with a fish inside that was crying:

"Stop it! Stop it!
I will fall!
I do not like this!
Not at all!"

The delegates cheered madly. I shuddered, expecting the worst. Though admittedly, the worst could not be as bad as it would have been before my capitulation to Clark. I shuddered, that is to say, and giggled a bit at the same time. Certainly, we had one helluva candidate.

The Cat was now doing a handstand on the skates, balancing the whole assemblage on his toes. He lifted one hand. Then he lifted the other. Down with a crash came Cat, Hat, rake, cake, goat, coat, umbrella, and bowl. The fishbowl hit the platform like a tidal wave. Suddenly the entire hall was engulfed. I was swimming for my life, far below the surface. Which was a miracle in itself, since I don't know how to swim. I don't even take deep baths. People floated by, some struggling, some laughing, some waving, some weeping, some winking, all making little bubbles that turtles, eels, and schools of peculiar fish swam through. Chairs passed. On one sat a little old lady delegate from New Hampshire, knitting as always. She glanced up, scowled at me over her spectacles. Placards. TV cameras. Ned, upside down, tangled in phone cords. Raccoons. Little Cat Hats. Riley passed, astride a catskinned co-ed: he tipped his hat politely and gave the victory sign.

I surfaced, gasping for breath. The goat bobbed by, riding his cake. I grabbed for the cake to save myself, got only a fistful of soggy frosting. I was going under again. My entire life passed, in melodramatic accord with that old wives' tale, before my eyes. It was full of brown suits, charred hamburger, political polls, income tax forms, exchanged gratuities, and unreadable newspapers: so dull, so insane, I spluttered, "I consider it a great honor!" and sank away. At which point, the fish, now grown to Leviathan size, appeared and swallowed me up.

I was not alone in the belly of the fish.

The whole damned National Convention was in there. Except the Cat and Clark. I was looking for Clark. This was too god-damned much. I'd nearly died. I was soaked, nauseous, exhausted, terrorized, enraged. "Clark!" I screamed. "Where the hell are you?" That vicious bastard. "Get us outa here, Clark!" My voice echoed and resounded in the fish's belly, mingling with the moans and cries of others.

A catskinned co-ed, hair dribbling down her face and cattail adroop, fell on my shoulder weeping. "There, there," I said. I patted her wet bottom. I began to feel a little better.

"Maybe he's Jesus," she whimpered.

"Now, now," I said, "we'll be all right."

All of us, even the raccoons, stayed huddled close together, grateful for each other's presence. A soft lamentation went up: what to do? who can save us? Sam remembered that in the morning TV cartoons they always used pepper. But nobody had any pepper. Then I recalled my crack about the great emetic. "Hey, Voom!" I said.

"Voom!" They all picked it up. "Voom!" they shouted. *"Voom! VOOM!"* The gates opened and we spewed forth.

I was rushing through the water at a tremendous speed. Luckily, we were all expelled outward in diverging directions: collision would have been fatal. I slowed, breathless, knocked up against a glass wall. I'd been clinging to my catskinned co-ed all the while, frantically patting her bottom to reassure myself. Or at least I'd thought it was hers—I was distressed to discover that in reality it belonged to my candidate Riley. I apologized confusedly. He tipped his straw politely and bobbed away.

I stared out through the glass wall. We seemed to be in the Convention hall, which was now enormously expanded—some trick, maybe, of the glass wall. Certainly, unless my eyes deceived me, it was concave. We seemed high up. I tried to make out what was just below us. It looked for all the world like a huge umbrella. And beneath that: the face of the Cat in the Hat grinning up at us. Swimmingly, monstrously distorted. We were, I realized, in the fishbowl. "Hang on!" I shouted to my-self and held my nose. And, sure enough, we fell.

We washed up on our own Convention hall benches. I seemed to hear the Cat's voice behind me the while:

> "Now you see
> What I can do!
> I can give you
> Something new!
> Something true
> And impromptu!
> I can give you
> A new view!"

"Up yours," said I, as I collapsed, gasping, into my chair. Phoo! Another round of that and I'm done for. It was about then I began thinking of getting out of politics. It wasn't the last time I was to have such thoughts. I felt my clothes; they were dry. I glanced around at the others. Everyone in a state of bug-eyed shock. That old New Hampshire grandmother was still knitting away, but she'd lost her yarn. Click, click. There was a moment of general recognition, a Convention-wide blink. Faint foolish smiles. When, now warily, we turned once more toward the Cat in the Hat, he was exiting, balanced on a ball, juggling hopelessly infatuated cat-skinned co-eds. Ned and Joe led us in singing "The Cat in the Hat Campaign Song" and "The Star-Spangled Banner." We had our candidates. The campaign was on.

That night, I found a fish in my pocket. Dead, I think. Anyway, I flushed it down the toilet. I was not just a little bit disgruntled, nor was I the only one. The Cat's contemptuous travesty of an acceptance of a Presidential nomination by one of the nation's two major political parties had shocked us all, even his wildest supporters. Oh, we were quick to rationalize it, give the world at large a happy line, and all the old Jonah jokes got revived, but there was the gloomy cautionary stink of seaweed in the air. The Cat was entertaining, maybe, exciting, liberating, even prodigious—but he was also, obscurely, a threat. Dangerous, yes, he was. He seemed to be in control of himself, but who could follow him without great personal peril? A whole nation in a fish's belly? No, we were in trouble. We all squeezed the *Me-You!* hats merrily and, with enthusiasm and the stirring sense of a great impending drama, went to bat for the Cat in the Hat, but, alone, we'd all found dead fish in our pockets and handbags.

I explained this that night to Clark. "Any great liberation is always accompanied by a vague sense of loss," he replied. "The structures we build to protect us from reality are insane, Mr. Brown, but they are also comforting. A false comfort, to be sure, but their loss is momentarily frightening."

"It's not going to get a lot of votes, Clark."

"You're still concerned about the elections, Mr. Brown."

"Hell, yes! Aren't you?"

Clark stared at me. I grew uneasy. "I believe, simply, that we live in an age of darkness, that humanity, with all efficiency and presumed purpose, has gone mad. What we must do, Mr. Brown, is help all men once more to experience reality concretely, fully, wholly, without mystification, free from mirages, unencumbered by pseudo-systems. If we succeed at that, don't you see, elections may no longer be relevant."

"That's what the goddamn fish's belly was all about, hunh?"

"Extremity is often a great catalyst, Mr. Brown. As a practicing politician, you must know that better than I."

I remembered the catskinned co-ed's sleek wet bottom, her warm tears, the sense of emptiness and community, the cavernous hollow of the fish's innards. A la Walt Disney, I realized, having cleaned a few fish in my time. Also, now that I thought about it, there was light in there. Where did it come from? Well, it didn't matter, it was a great show, I had to admit it, I'd never see things the same way again, find your soul in the Cat's fishbowl, and briefly, before I remembered its sliminess, I even appreciated the dead fish I'd found in my pocket.

Then I recalled that old lady clicking her empty knitting needles. "It's a pipe dream, Clark. People aren't built for it. Call it insanity, if you like. I call it survival."

"But who is surviving, Mr. Brown? We are engaged in brutal wars, we live in the shadow of thermonuclear world-death, we continue to exist by virtue of dead forms, cut off from all life, from all being, as much murderers as survivors . . . and then we all die anyway."

I stared at Clark. He was intense, assertive, ugly. He radiated concern and engagement. And he knew too much about loneliness. "Say, listen, Clark, tell me: do you have a single goddamn friend in the world?"

"Certainly, Mr. Brown. You." I was sorry I had asked. "You're not quitting, are you?"

I sighed. I was close to it that night. "No, but, nutty or not, I'd sure as hell like to win this election."

"Who says we won't?"

"Well, I tell you, it'd sure help if you

could get the Cat to act just a little more
. . . well . . . normal."

That incipient smile flickered over Clark's
face. I grinned openly in return, went out
for a couple platesful of hamburger steak,
done to a bloodless crisp. I was starved.

The Cat was a phenomenal campaigner
. . . if that was what he was doing. Tire-
less, astounding, unpredictable, he was lit-
erally everywhere at once, plummeting out
of airplanes, umbrella for a parachute, over
Butte and Baltimore, popping up out of
sewers in Hyannis and Williamsburg,
whistle-stopping from Cucamonga to Santa
Monica, flying kites in Houston and drop-
ping confetti on Bedford-Stuyvesant, set-
ting up a freak show in the valleys at
Gettysburg, bathing in the Chicago River
and brushing his teeth in Hot Springs, ped-
dling boxes and foxes to passersby in Old
Rampart, Alaska, giving away life insur-
ance in San Francisco, eating grits in
Spokane and knishes in Biloxi. He juggled
live bears in Yellowstone, spaceships in
Florida, dialects in New York. He fell off

Pike's Peak, doing a handstand on a cane and a vane, and washed up on a door with an oar off Kailua Bay, singing Happy Birthday songs.

But if he was unpredictable, he was also unmanageable. I made the mistake the first couple weeks of arranging speaking engagements for him—the Cat missed them all, popping up at the Opponent's rallies instead. The Opponent, political genius and campaign veteran though he was, was at as much of a loss as Boone or I had been at our Convention. I admit I was secretly pleased to see the sonuvabitch discomfited, but I couldn't go along with Clark's claim that the Cat's goofy gambits were exposing the madness of normalcy. Okay, I realize the Opponent—Mr. America, his party's buttons and posters called him—was guilty of all the old clichés about "free enterprise" and "government of the people, by the people, and for the people" and "unalienable rights" and "the American Way of Life" and "defense of freedom" and "government is a business and should be run like one," all the usual crap, but what the hell, that's pragmatic politics, that's winning elections, that's talking the tribal language, and it's not what Clark liked to call "our national depravity." And sure, the Cat's playback of these old saws in his singsong ditties did make them sound pretty nutty. "This Wee of Life is rife with strife!" he'd singalong. And:

> "Some laws are no!
> Some laws are yes!
> All flaws are good
> For bus-i-ness!
>
> Some laws are may!
> Some laws are must!
> The Mannikin Way:
> In God we rust!"

Or he'd carry that "government of the people" jazz out to "until the people, down the people, between the people, across the people, past the people, into the people, round the people, beyond the people, since the people," and so on to "government up

the people." That always brought the house
down, but I wonder if the Cat ever knew
why. I mean, he just didn't seem to have
that kind of mind. If he had any mind at all.

Clark was convinced the Opponent was
mad. And therefore his party was mad. And
in fact any nation that could seriously consider for President a man who, for example,
in Paterson and Cleveland promised vast
federal programs "to liberate our great
cities, once and for all, from misery, suffering, and despair," and in Phoenix and
Mobile championed states' rights and re-
duced taxes, and embraced the local gov-
ernors, was ipso facto a crazed and stricken
society. His pet phrase was "biologically
dysfunctional." As far as I was concerned,
it only showed Clark knew a lot less about
people and politics than he liked to think.
It even bothered him that the Opponent was
a Mason, kept dogs, went to baseball games,
taught Sunday School, watched TV, and
played golf, especially when he learned that
the Opponent didn't especially *like* to play
golf.

It's true, the Opponent made a pretty bad showing against the Cat, even blew his wig a couple times, but what would you do if you stood to address your fellow party members at a five-hundred-dollar-a-plate dinner and discovered it was nothing but a stable full of braying polka-dotted donkeys wearing Cat Hats? What would you do if you got into a nationally televised VIP Golf Tournament and found yourself up against a silly Cat in a floppy Hat who swished eight-foot-long rubbery clubs at skittery golf balls with eyes and noses and got holes-in-one, while your own clubs oddly weighed a ton all of a sudden and kept sticking into the ground and taking root? What would your comeback be if, while addressing a national convention of the American Legion on the primacy of patriotism, your clothes suddenly fell off you ("defoliation," my friend Sam quipped in a speech in Minneapolis), leaving you diapered in Old Glory, noticeably soiled? What the Opponent said was: "This is an outrage!" And indeed it was.

The Cat's first encounter with the Opponent set the pace for the entire campaign, as long as the Opponent lasted anyway. The Opponent's party had selected the American eagle as its election-year symbol to go along with the Mr. America idea, and the Cat arrived flapping in on one, a huge, shaggy, cross-eyed, baldheaded beast, surely the dumbest bird I've ever seen. The Opponent had just finished lifting his right hand and saying, "With God's help and yours . . ." when the whole apparition descended upon him. The bird, clutching a popgun and a jar of olives in its claws, landed square on its face, tumbling pell-mell across the stage with the Cat in the Hat, knocking over the lectern, upending lights and cameras, smearing the Opponent's TV makeup, shitting frantically on everything and everybody, and sending olives bounding around the place like pinballs. The bird stumbled clumsily to its feet in a tangle of wires, yuk-yukking giddily, shot itself in the eye with the popgun, and staggered around the stage, trampling right over the bewildered Opponent. The Cat leaped up to conduct the orchestra in playing the National Anthem backwards, the stupid eagle clucking raucously like an old hen through the whole performance and holding up a sign that read: MAKE AMERICA SAFE FOR DEMOCRACY! The Opponent, besmeared, trampled, splattered with eagle shit, staggered desperately to the microphone to call a halt to the travesty, but when he grabbed hold of it, it turned into Ned dressed up like Liberty. *"RAPE!"* he/she shrieked, and four burly cops rushed onstage to haul off, kicking and bawling like a baby, Mr. America.

Needless to say, the Opponent's poll ratings fell off pretty sharply after that. Under his picture in the papers the next day: *Can't Cat-chup!* The press was having a field day and the Cat seemed to have the election in the bag. The Feline in the Felt, they called him, Tom in the Tam, the Magic Mouser, King Kitten, the Tabby in the Topper, the Peerless Puss, the Magnifi-Cat, the Chief Exekitty. They loved him, couldn't get

enough, ran whole special editions on the
trips he took them on. A lot of it was due
simply to the power of sensationalism—
who'd ever done what he was doing?—but
also, I had to admit it, we were all hungry
for some good fun, tired of war and all our
private miseries, sick of the old clichés,
the bomb scare and the no exits, in the
mood for extravagance and whimsy ("Tom-
foolery," the press labeled it); there was a
long-repressed belly-laugh rumbling deep
in the collective gut, and the Cat was loosing
it. Clark called it a kind of exorcism, and I
had to agree. "We'll rid you yet, Mr. Brown,
of all those troublesome 'vectors,'" he
added, and since against all logic and my
own instincts, we were winning, I only
grinned and supposed it might be so.

Frankly, I still couldn't grasp the Cat's
success, and my acceptance of it was something like a leap of faith. I'd watched the
American people vote for several decades,
and though I was beginning to get a feel of
their almost hysterical delight in what Clark
called "freedom," I still couldn't see them

soberly pulling that lever for the Cat in the Hat, come November. Nevertheless, I had come along some since the Convention. I'd even bought myself a red-and-white striped tie. The middle of a frenetic Convention hall floor is an awkward place from which to look out on the world, which is probably why, from there, I was sure we were making a big mistake. I just couldn't imagine those people out there getting excited about that zany Cat. A Convention hall is like a lot of mirrors: you're looking at yourself looking out at them looking in at you looking at yourself, and so on, until finally there aren't any lookers or objects, just looking itself, which is to say, nothing at all. "Our cate-chumen in catoptrics," Clark once jokingly called me, and he had his point. Then, once the campaign had actually begun, I began to pick up new sounds, new signs, new motions. Yes, the Cat was touching something, some forgotten nerve, and some-thing was happening. Testimonials were coming in. Not just from nuts, but also from plain Americans—grocers, housewives, doc-

tors, carpenters. They liked the Cat. They
were going to bat for him. They believed
in him. They wanted him to go to Russia
and China as soon as he was elected and
talk to the people there. Where could you
buy a set of those rubbery golf clubs? Was
the clean-up machine patented?

"Be careful, Mr. Brown," Clark cau-
tioned me when I talked about the testimonials. "There are no plain Americans.
And there's much more yet to happen."

"Listen, Clark, don't screw things up
now. I mean it. This can be something great,
but we're not there yet."

"No, that's true, Mr. Brown. And neither
are you."

I let it pass. I was feeling too good. An
election I couldn't win, and somehow we
were winning it. In fact, I got a lot of com-
pliments about it. I came to understand that
the whole nation was in a defeatist mood,
just like our party, so that our Convention
was like a microcosmic image, a preview,
of what was now happening across the
country. As for the magic, well, an age of

wild scientific leaps is well-conditioned to accept amazements. I'm sure everybody, just like me, expected to find out later how it was all done. Some new formula, no doubt, that nobody would understand but everybody could accept.

Though not as funny maybe, the Cat's most devastating act came during his and the Opponent's first—and last—nationally televised debate. The Opponent appeared, wearing his familiar small-town brown fedora, and began to speak of his pioneer grandfathers, one a blacksmith, the other a prairie preacher. The Cat suddenly interrupted: "Off with your hat, please!" The hat flew off, and under it was found to be a banker's bowler. The Opponent, as though unaware of what was happening, continued his speech without a pause, but now he was talking about investment credits, the threat of peace and depression, and "dynamic" solutions to "the problems of inventory." "Off with your hat, please!" said the Cat in the Hat. The bowler flew off and there was a biretta. Now it was "soldiers of Christ" and "the Prince of Peace" and the menace of "atheistic materialism" and "families that pray together—"which got interrupted again by the Cat's command. Off flew the biretta, revealing a wide-banded golfer's straw, and the Opponent switched abruptly from Christian pieties to locker-room banter and a really awful story about a guy with piles. This was followed by a miner's helmet, a fraternity pledge cap, a periwig, a pith hat, a *yarmulke*, a football helmet, beret, ten-gallon hat, mortarboard, earmuffs, Marine general's cap, nightcap, morion, a half-collapsed beaver, a black billycock, a cowl, a crown, a feather, a flower. The Opponent rattled on insanely, now a jungle fighter, now a hippie, next a cop hollering for law and order, then a farmer shooting pigs, a sociologist discussing the "territorial imperative," a dry-goods salesman trying to make out in the big city. At last it was all running together in one mad gibberish of sound, hats flying off his head like a string of rockets, until —suddenly—he seemed to swallow his tongue; off flew the last hat, a dunce cap, revealing: the Cat's Hat, of course. In the sudden silence, he reached up and pinched it. *ME-YOU!* It convulsed the house, ended the debate, all but ended the campaign. The Opponent sat there in the Hat, giggling idiotically, squeezing it spasmodically. There was, in fact, talk afterward about committing him to an institution, which would have caused a terrific international scandal, but the Cat generously undertook his reconstruction, beginning all over with the ABC's and a bunch of other letters the Cat had thought up. The Opponent, in turn, simply retired from the public scene. This was about the end of September. A poll then revealed the Cat was assured of roughly 87 percent of the vote. The other 13 percent was uncommitted. It looked to be an electoral college whitewash.

In retrospect, I realize that, although the Opponent got shot down mainly by the Cat, the Cat's own complementary rise was mainly the work of people like Sam and Ned and Joe. And myself, if you don't

mind. Not only did the Cat's acts insist on
a lot of interpreting ("Well, what the Cat's
trying to say, you see, is that things aren't
always what they seem, life is unpredictable, and so to thine own self be true, because you can fool all of the people some
of the time and some of the people all of
the time, but not . . . yes, that's right,
now you're getting it . . ."), but after suffering through a couple of his spectacles,
people simply needed the reassurance of
other normal human beings around them,
even if Clark was right, and we were *all*
really out of our minds. Ned and Joe, in
fact, virtually ignored the Cat after the Convention, running their own show quite apart
from him, at least as much as they could;
you couldn't always depend on the Cat stay-
ing away. I sometimes wondered if those
two guys really had the faintest idea who or
what their candidate was, but I have to
admit, I needed the familiar as much as
anyone else, and so found comfort in their
traditional barnstorm tactics. Ned operated
mainly in the Midwest, Joe in the South and

Southwest, though they often reenacted their Convention soft-shoe routines together.

My job, as I saw it, was to keep the party regulars in line, and given the Cat's irreverent antics, they were pretty nervous, so it was a full-time job. He projected all our Chicago ward bosses right through the Planetarium dome one evening, for example, and kept them in orbit for seven days before soft-landing them in a Zen Buddhist monastery in the Sierra Nevada, where, every time they asked how to get to Chicago, a Zen master would slap their faces or dump bowls of porridge on their heads. Two of them came back with flowers in their hair, but the rest of them, quite naturally, wanted to quit. I reminded them that the Cat was sweeping the country, that that very stunt in fact had added another three percent to the Cat's advantage, that this was no time to get off the winning team, and I even, with great difficulty, managed to get Honorary Astronaut medals for them. They stayed.

But it was Sam, more than any of us,

who carried Clark's special message to the world—deflected, of course, through a professional politician's caution, but for that, the easier to swallow. While Clark argued that our national inertia was the impermissible product of praxis, for example, Sam merely suggested that we needn't suppose the status quo was necessarily either natural or ordained by God, but, since we were free men, we could try to make life into something fresh and new and beautiful. Clark wanted an immediate total-population recognition of the full spectrum of personal and social options; Sam indicated ways we might improve things on earth by working together. He did well, especially in the East and Northwest, and on college campuses. I began to see him as our Presidential candidate four years from now. I was still thinking in those terms. In fact, I confess, I found myself wishing more than once that he was our candidate right now, and not merely running for the Vice-Presidency.

One night, between stops in an airport

bar in Albuquerque, Sam going one way
and me the other, I asked him: "Well, how's
it gonna feel to be Vice-President?"

"What?"

"Vice-President. You're running for
Vice-President, you know."

He smiled. "I don't know if I'm running
*for any*thing, Sooth. Sometimes it seems
like what it's all about is the running itself."

"I know what you mean. The trouble
with the democratic process is that the campaigns are too much fun, the jobs themselves too goddamn boring. Those two years
I spent in Congress were the worst years of
my life."

"That's not exactly what I meant. I mean,
I think the Cat is carrying us out past
ordinary space-time notions, out to something new where these old ways of identify-
ing ourselves will seem sad and empty."

"I've had that feeling, too, Sam. Sometimes I think there aren't going to be any
actual elections in November, that instead
this goddamn thing is going to just keep on
expanding and expanding, until taking an

actual vote is going to be about as meaningful as pausing to pick a flower in a stam-
pede."

"Are you worried about it, Sooth?"

"Goddamn right. It scares the hell out of
me to think of no elections four years from
now and eight years from now, just like
I'm scared to die. I'm a coward, Sam.
Pussy-lanimous Brown. There's one for your
fucking Cat."

Sam laughed. "Sooth, you're still holding back, you're still not with us. Come on,
jump in, something's happening, something
great!"

"I wonder if the Opponent would agree
with you there."

"Sure he would! He does!"

"His wife doesn't."

"Sooth, it hurts to heal. Give her time.
We've been living in a shutdown world.
We're opening it up. It's worth it."

"You've been hanging around old Clark
too much. Listen, he's a bright boy, but he's
all mixed up about the psyche. He thinks
you can do anything with it, that it's es-

sentially empty and formless, you just have
to realize it and presto! a new world. Well,
people with psyches like that aren't the
people I know. I don't even know newborn
babies like that. I'll tell you what the human
constant is, Sam, and you should know it
as well as I, it's that big fat immovable
mass, the old muddle-of-the-roaders, most
of them programmed the wrong way from
birth, all of them stuck to the earth with
hungers and sex grabs, scared to die or even
get hurt, encumbered with defects and
damages, and essentially inert even when
they look like they're moving." They'd
called Sam's plane in the middle of my
harangue, and I ended up shouting it at
him past the gates. "And, listen, Sam, take
it easy! Don't get overcommitted! When
this Cat thing's over, you're it! You hear?
You're it, Sam! Don't get screwed up!"

The next night, Sam appeared on television. Sam was good on television, had
just the right soft-sell manner. But that night
the Cat showed up. It wasn't the first time.
He was nearly as hard on us as he was on

the Opponent. You could never be sure he entirely understood we were on his side. Sam knew what to do when the Cat turned up: he just got out of the silly bastard's way. Ned and Joe and some of the others weren't always so smart and usually ended up paying the consequences, suffering the whole course of sleight-of-mind exhibitions with the rest of the hapless populace. This night, the Cat went so far as to leap past Sam and bounce out of every television set in the nation, dragging with him the whole kit and caboodle of commercial TV: spies, cowboys, comics, pitchmen, sob-sisters, cops, preachers, aviators, gumshoes, crooners, talking animals, quarterbacks, and panelists, the whole daffy lot parading through all the bedrooms, living rooms, dens, and bars of the country, shooting it up, wisecracking, blowing whistles, asking irrelevant questions, beating people up. It was pretty unsettling, and a lot of sets got turned off for awhile after that.

At the time, of course, I didn't know

about everybody else getting it, too. I thought it was just me he was after. I thought maybe he'd found out about that conversation I'd had with Sam in Albuquerque. I was in a hotel in Zanesville, Ohio. The set in my room was an old one, and I had a hard time focusing Sam in. He kept splitting off diagonally. But I'd finally got it adjusted and had just settled back in an armchair with a cold drink, had my shoes off and was rubbing my toes, when—wham!—there was the Cat leaping out of there, followed by a hockey team from Montreal, a daisy chain of elephants out of a documentary on India, a boxcar of dead American G.I.'s, plus three motorcycle cops, a chorus line, the Olympic swimming team, a mean kid in a toy fire engine, three unwed mothers, and a used-car salesman. A lot more came, but I didn't see them, because a stagecoach and horses rolled right down a mountainside into the room and over me. When I came to, I found myself stripped naked, right down to my fuzzy pot belly and old pale thighs, surrounded by a horde of teenyboppers from a dance-band show, the audience from a panel game, and the entire membership of the Mickey Mouse Club, and being poked in the privates by a TV medic. "Hmmm," he was saying solemnly, "looks like we'll have to operate." "Hey! Cut that out!" I hollered. "You're nothing but an *actor!*" And for some goddamn reason they all laughed at that till they cried.

Well, I was sore, and when I heard about the incredible scope of the act, I guessed I wasn't alone. I saw trouble ahead. We got it. The very next day, there was the Cat in the Hat, raining pink ink all over a hostile confrontation of whites and blacks in Jacksonville. Very funny, but it didn't go over in Jacksonville, since it turned out both sides had been spoiling for that fight for a long time. And the Cat's ambivalent blackness, heretofore a political asset, now turned on him: he was suddenly an upstart nigger to whites, a Tom to blacks. Moreover, peo-

through all the churches in Indianapolis, crying:

> "Look at me!
> Look at me!
> Look at me NOW!
> It is fun to have fun
> But you have to know how!"

I rushed in on Clark. "Stop him before it's too late!" I cried.

"Too late for what, Mr. Brown?"

I showed him the latest poll. The Cat was down to sixty-one percent. Which, with no visible opponent, was anything but overwhelming. "See? You've been wrong, Clark!"

"Wrong? Why, not at all, Mr. Brown." Clark's calm was spine-shaking. "Oh, by the way, look at this letter we've just received."

I snatched it up. Oakland postmark. "Hey, man, your krazy kat turns me on wow like next time try the late late show send me old lionel barrymoor in a wheelchair I want to turn him on, man, I mean put me in orbit with carol lombard and I'll go to bat, man, I really will! *Me-yeah!*" I threw it down in disgust. "Aw, goddamn it, Clark, that's just some hippie! He probably won't even bother to vote!"

"So?" The hint of a smile flickered across Clark's pale face. "Now, don't pout like that, Mr. Brown."

It was hopeless. I stalked out. And the next day, while Joe was speaking in Washington on the importance of military preparedness ("Only the strong and the brave are free!"), the Cat arrived on a tricycle, blowing a rusty fife, raised the Pentagon off the ground, and spun it like a top—hilarious to disaffected potheads maybe, but not to the Joint Chiefs of Staff, all of whom in their cold commitment ended up in Walter Reed Hospital. Played havoc with all the Pentagon computers, too, a pretty penny and a lot of history shot to hell.

Well, that did it. Within hours we had received rumors and then anonymous confirmation of an Army-centered takeover plot, and shortly after, we got that other phone call, telling us that the so-called moderate wing of our party—which in reality was just about everybody—was pulling out to support the Opponent.

So the situation that afternoon was this: (1) if the Cat in the Hat threatened to win, and to be sure he still had over fifty percent of the people behind him, the Army would pull their coup the week before elections and install the Opponent as President pro tem, until a new Constitutional Convention could be held; and (2), whether the Opponent won more or less legally or by fiat, we were faced with the prospect of a driveling idiot for President, the virtual political bankruptcy of our party and thus of the American two-party system, and personal lifelong ignominy for each of us.

"A military takeover? Here in the United States?" Sam had asked disbelievingly on answering the earlier call. "Easiest thing in the world," the voice on the other end had replied. Calmly. Coolly. Sam said after, he'd heard the rattle of hospital carts and trays. And true: it no doubt was easy. Who could stop them if they wanted to do it?

> "I can stop them
> With my tricks!
> With my kicks
> And pricks and sticks!"

We stared at the Cat. He sat there in that floppy striped Hat, parody of Uncle Sam's, gloved hands folded over his skinny chest, grinning that silly grin. What about it? Tip the media, expose the generals' plans? Pull a counter-coup? But who'd be with us? That freak from Oakland maybe. I envied old Riley and Boone their way out.

"Could he do it, Clark?" Sam asked softly.

Clark was staring at us intensely. I'm sure, if it had been pitch dark, we could have seen his glowing eyes. "Why not?" he said. "Dismantling of a few outmoded systems, like the military, the Cabinet, police and espionage organiza—"

"Jesus Christ, Clark!" Joe blurted out

angrily. "You're talking about a total violent disruption, man!"

"Of course." That fierce burning gaze. "What did you think this was?"

"But what would we *do* without an army?" Ned asked incredulously.

"Let's try it and find out."

"Now, goddamn it, Clark—!"

"But wait, Clark," Sam interceded, "doesn't a nation in a world like ours *need* a good defense system? I mean, I know what you've been saying about the debasement and insanity of machine-like military and production systems, but how else can we survive as a society?"

"What's more important? Physical survival of an accidental human horde or idea survival? So what if nations more barbarian than ours defeat us militarily? Probably we should just lie down and let them come. Because sooner or later, they'll get it, the exemplary message will sink in—"

"Ohh shiitt!" Joe moaned softly.

And then that phone call from the rump group of benedict moderates came, the Cat got booted out, I talked Sam as heir-apparent into absenting himself, and we sat down to some really serious talk. "All right, Sooth, we're listening," Ned said.

A week later, the Cat appeared at a rally outside a small town in Mississippi, along the banks of the Pearl River. We had alerted the personnel of a nearby airbase, the White Citizens Council and the Black Nationalists, the local Minutemen, Klan, Nazis, Black Muslims, and Zionists, the National Guard and the VFW, the different student groups, the local churches, sheriffs, shopkeepers, cops, Mafia interests, farmers, Cubans, Choctaws, country singers, and evangelists, in short, all the Good Folk of the valley. Our precautions were hardly necessary—the same thing would have happened in Walla Walla or Concord by then —but it was only a week before the threatened coup, and since the Cat had a habit of skipping out on scheduled appearances, we were pretty nervous about it. By flattery, cajolery, and just plain hanging on to him, we kept him in sight until we could get him on the scene. Even Clark helped, though I'll never know why exactly.

That they'd kill him, we knew. That they'd do it by skinning him alive we hadn't foreseen, but those folks along the Pearl are pretty straightforward people. I guess we'd been around him too long and had begun to forget he was a cat. Another thing we hadn't counted on was Sam's showing up. I knew he was upset about the thing but I thought I'd convinced him to stay away. I have my flaw, I've told you about it, and Sam had his: he believed in reason. He came there to *talk* to those people, for Christ's sake! Oh, poor sweet Sam! "Violence solves nothing!" he cried out, standing in front of the Cat, and somebody shot him in the head. Right between the eyes. Clark talks about reality. Nothing has ever been nor ever will be so real to me as that sick disbelieving expression on Sam's face the instant before the hole opened up. I was backing away, but I came up against a solid wall of people. There was no getting through.

They tied the Cat's feet together and hung him over a peg pounded into the upright beam of a tall cross. He put up no resistance, merely smiled benignly through it all. Oddly, though he was upside down, his Hat did not fall off. For some reason, this enraged the crowd. They all gave a pull on it, including a huge black man, said to be the strongest sonuvabitch this side of the Yazoo. But it wouldn't give. They kicked the Cat in the face, spat on him, punched his belly with pig-stickers, slammed his balls with the blunt end of an ax. But the Hat stayed on. And the Cat just smiled back at them, blinking his long lashes, twiddling his thumbs.

They'd apparently decided on a simple slaying, and a wizened 107-year-old redneck from up in Sunflower County had been handed the knife, but, their blood boiling now, they all went after him with whatever they had at hand, switchblades, hatpins, goads, hatchets, scissors, rusty razor blades. "That is that," the Cat in the Hat was heard to say, and they closed in. There was a mad frenzy of pulling and ripping, cursing and gut-flinging, and they weren't too neat maybe, but it was a thorough job of skinning a cat. Except for the Hat: when they were done, it was still there. And the gloved hands, still folded over a now glistening pink chest. And the placid grin, though now a bit macabre. Ned, Joe, and I, unable to break free, had pulled together. Clark, we noticed, had disappeared.

The crowd stood around now, panting, staring at the dead cat, still dissatisfied somehow. There was a lot of corn liquor getting passed around. Survival, Clark, that's what it's all about, goddamn it, I was saying to myself. Fuck your revelations, I want outa here! About then, somebody thought of matches. As I recall, it was a little kid, about eight years old. They heaped up leaves and old newspapers at the foot of the cross, tossed on the Cat's skin. They were about to light it, when a fat black woman slipped up timidly and dropped her kerchief on the pile. An old sunburned farmer pulled off his straw sun hat, hesitated, then tossed it on. Someone kicked off his boots and pitched them forward. A cop threw his belt on. A man pulled off his shirt. A woman unzipped her dress. A youngster tore off his pants. Before I could grasp what was happening, the whole mob was stark naked. Joe and Ned and I stood out like the strangers we were. Not for long: they jumped us, hogtied us over tree branches, cut our clothes off us, and threw them on the now mountainous pile, put the match to it all.

What followed was a pretty marvelous orgy, spoiled only by the stink of all those burning rags and the pall Sam cast, and I regretted that my situation forced me to play such a passive role in it. While the Cat burned, the throng fucked in a great conglobation of races, sexes, ages, and convictions; it was the Great American Dream in oily actuality, and magically, every time an orifice was newly probed, it uttered the *Me-You!* Cat-Call.

Nor was the Cat in the Hat done with us.

His roasted corpse was rescued from the flames, ripped apart, and passed around. I objected, but to no avail, and the burnt flesh was jammed down my throat, ruining forever my taste for charred hamburger. Then . . . VOOM!

Now, I've smoked pot, chewed peyote, and even with an F.B.I. investigative team tripped once on LSD, but the Cat's meat was truly something else. For one thing, like the Cat himself, the vision was all red, white, and blue, shot through with stars, bars, and silver bullets. The whole hoopla of American history stormed through our exploded minds, all the massacres, motherings, couplings, and connivings, all the baseball games, PTA meetings, bloodbaths, old movies, and piracies. We lived through gold-digging, witch-burning, lumberjacking, tax-collecting, and barn-raising. Presidents and prophets fought for rostrums by the dozens. We saw everything, from George Washington reading the graffiti while straining over a constipated shit in Middlebrook,

New Jersey, to Teddy Roosevelt whaling
his kids, from Johnson and Kennedy shooting it out on a dry dusty street in a deserted
cowtown to Ben Franklin getting struck by
lightning while jacking off on a rooftop
in Paris. It was all there, I can't begin to
tell it, all the flag-waving, rip-staving, truck-
driving, gun-toting, ram-squaddled, ring-
tail-roaring, bronc-breaking, A-bombing,
drag-racing, Christ-kissing, bootlegging,
coffee-drinking, pig-fucking tale of it all.
And through it all, I kept catching glimpses
of the Cat in the Hat, gunning Japs out of
the sky over Hollywood, humping B'rer
Rabbit's tar-baby, giving Custer what-for at
Little Big Horn, pulling aces out of his
sleeves in New Orleans; now he was in a
peruke signing the Declaration of Inde-
pendence with a ballpoint pen, then in a
sou'wester going down with the *Maine*, next
leaping with a smirk and a daisy in his
teeth out of the President's box onto the
stage of Ford's Theater, inventing the cotton
gin, stoking Casey Jones' fires, lopping off

heads at Barnegat with Captain Kidd, boo-hooing with Sam Tilden and teeing off with Bing Crosby.

Too much, and the effect finally wasn't so much entertainment as mere exhaustion, and I wonder now, sitting here in my Attorney General's office in Washington, if the Cat's whole act wasn't mainly to leave you just sitting quietly, staring blankly out a window, with an empty mind and a body gratefully at rest. Those good Pearl River folks were so tuckered, it was all they could do to smear a little tar on our hind ends, slap on a handful of chicken feathers, and prod us, if not out of the county, at least up the road a little piece.

The Cat in the Hat as candidate was a national calamity; as martyr, he took us to the White House. His death shocked the nation. Sam's should have, but no one paid much attention to it; it was like a normal and almost proper supporting casualty. I wept like a goddamn baby about it. I kept seeing Sam's gentle face with that hole in it.

I blamed the Cat. For a couple of weeks, Mississippi was policed by federal troops. The F.B.I. investigated. Our party reconvened solemnly in Philadelphia, where, after stirring tributes to the Cat in the Hat from leaders of every political persuasion, Riley was nominated for President with Boone as his running mate. Our central platform promise was "The New View." The Cat's Hat became a somber symbol, the Cat-Call a moving chant, the Campaign Song a kind of party hymn. Ned penned a new rhyme—he thought of it merely as a last-minute campaign slogan, but it was eventually to enter the American canon, immortalizing that one-time St. Louis shoe salesman . . .

> "Do not fear!
> The Cat is here!
> Where?
> There!
> Near?
> Here!
> There and here!

> Here and there!
> The Cat in the Hat
> Is EVERYWHERE!"

We won in a walk, a cat-walk, as Joe and Ned might have it, backed by the military, labor, Wall Street, the press, the peace movement, Negroes, and the National Society for the Prevention of Cruelty to Animals. President Riley, as his first act of office, declared October 31 as Cat in the Hat Day. What about Sam's day? I asked. He shrugged. The Imperial Grand Wizard of the Ku Klux Klan turned the Cat's Hat over to the National Cat in the Hat Museum and Library in Princeton, New Jersey. Was it the real hat, or just a campaign forgery? Who can tell? Certainly no magic has come of it. Joe, I might mention, is now Undersecretary of State for Latin-American Affairs, and Ned is with Bell Telephone.

Ironically, one of my jobs as Attorney General is to keep under constant surveillance my old friend Clark, who is in effect, though he may not be aware of it, under a kind of permanent house arrest; well, that's politics. Legend has it, it's he who has the real Cat's Hat, and that inside it are twenty-six other Cats, ready to be sprung on an unsuspecting world. Oh boy. And where will we go then, Sam, where'll we go?